The School Carnival

Library of Congress Cataloging-in-Publication Data

Dobson, Danae.
   The school carnival / by Danae Dobson ; illustrated by Karen Loccisano.
     p. cm. — (The Sunny Street Kids' Club ; 4)
   "Word kids!"
   Summary: Conner learns what it means to "love your enemies" when three bullies
determine that he and his friends will fail to win the prize for the best booth.
   ISBN 0–8499–5115–1
   [1. Contests—Fiction. 2. Bullies—Fiction. 3. Christian life—Fiction.]   I. Title. II.
Series: Dobson, Danae.   Sunny Street Kids' Club ; 4.
   PZ7.D6614Sc   1996
   [Fic]—dc20   95–42264
                                                       CIP
                                                       AC

Printed in Hong Kong

96 97 98 99 00 PLP 9 8 7 6 5 4 3 2 1

The School Carnival

by
Danae Dobson

Illustrated by Karen Loccisano

WORD PUBLISHING
Dallas·London·Vancouver·Melbourne

Connor Riley and his friends giggled in the back of the classroom. His fourth-grade teacher told everyone to be quiet.

"All right, class," said Mr. Kelly, "I have an announcement. Next week is our school carnival. One of the sponsors is giving a one-hundred-dollar prize for creating the best booth. If any of you would like to participate, sign up before you leave today."

Connor turned to his friends Matthew, Lauren, and Stephanie.

"Did you hear that?" Connor whispered. "A one-hundred-dollar prize!"

"Yeah, and our club could sure use the money," said Lauren.

"Let's try to win!" said Matthew.

Just then, the bell rang. Connor hurried to the front of the classroom to sign up for the event. But before he could write down his name, he heard a voice behind him.

"Don't even try, Connor Riley—you can't win anything."

Connor turned to see three other students— Trevor, Ronnie, and Zach—standing behind him.

"What did you say?" asked Connor.

"You heard me," said Trevor. "Your silly club isn't going to win the prize—we are!"

"Oh, yeah?" said Connor. "We'll just see about that!"

The three boys smirked and walked away.

"Hey, Connor, forget about them," said Matthew. "Let's go to your house and have a club meeting."

That afternoon the children met in Connor's basement. Connor's six-year-old brother, Ryan, was there, as well as the club's mascot—the Riley's golden retriever, Rusty.

"All right, everyone, the Sunny Street Kids' Club is now in session," said Connor.

"Let's talk about the carnival next Saturday. Does anyone have an idea for a booth?"

"Well," said Stephanie, "We could have a puppet show or something."

"That's not creative," said Lauren. "There will probably be at least two other puppet shows at the carnival."

"I have an idea," said Matthew. "My Uncle Mike used to work at a circus, and he has an Orbotron. Maybe we could borrow it."

"An Orbotron?" asked Connor. "What's that?"

"It's shaped like a big globe," said Matthew, "and you strap a person in it and spin them around. It's a lot of fun."

"Now that's creative!" said Lauren. "We could charge a dollar a ride and make a ton of money!"

"That settles it," said Connor. "As your club president, I say we bring the Orbotron to the carnival."

"Wait! Wait!" said Ryan, raising his hand, "Matthew hasn't asked his uncle yet—what if he won't let us use it?"

"I'll call my uncle tonight," said Matthew. "And then I'll tell you at school tomorrow."

The next morning, Matthew had good news—his uncle had agreed to let them borrow his Orbotron.

Connor was so excited! "We're going to have the best booth at the carnival!" he said to Matthew.

Connor and his friends were quiet about their plan at school for the next few days. They didn't want anyone to know—especially Trevor, Ronnie, and Zach! The three boys had been teasing the Kids' Club and making rude comments.

But it got worse as the carnival drew near. Connor and his friends were walking home from school when a water balloon flew through the air and splattered behind them. Matthew's pants were soaking wet!

Connor saw three heads peeking out from behind a bush. He ran toward the boys, but they were gone by the time he got there.

Later that evening, Connor told his parents what had happened.

"I just don't understand it, Dad," said Connor. "We've never done anything to those guys, but they're so mean to us."

"Yes," said Mr. Riley. "There are people in this world who just want to cause trouble. But that doesn't mean we should act the same way."

"Remember what Jesus said in the Bible verse we memorized?" asked Mrs. Riley. "In Matthew 5:43-44, He said, 'There is a saying, "Love your friends and hate your enemies." But, I say, love your enemies! Pray for those who persecute you!'"

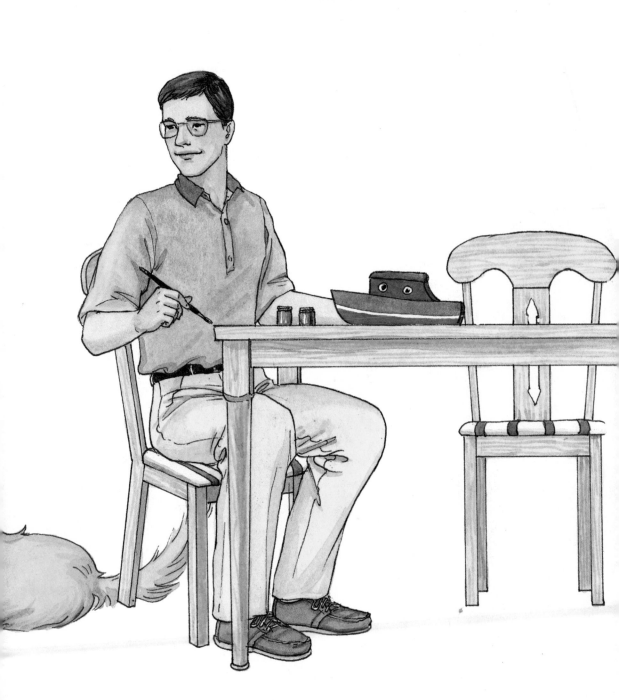

"So you see, Connor, Jesus wants us to show love to everyone—even those mean kids at school," added Mr. Riley.

"I'll try, but it isn't easy," said Connor. He gave his parents a hug and hurried off to bed.

The next morning when Connor and Ryan got to
school, they saw a big banner that read, "Hillside
Elementary School Carnival." Connor and Ryan
couldn't believe how different the playground looked!

They saw clowns, puppeteers, and magicians.
There was a petting zoo, a jungle jump, and even a
dunk tank!

"This is awesome," said Connor. "There are games and balloons all over the place!"

"Food, too!" said Ryan, glancing at the hot dog stand.

Mrs. Riley gave her sons a few dollars. "I'll be back to pick you up at four o'clock," she said.

"Come on!" said Connor, pulling on Ryan's arm. "Let's find the rest of the gang!"

Before long, they saw Stephanie and Lauren buying snow cones. Then the boys found Matthew and his Uncle Mike setting up the Orbotron.

"Wow!" said Connor, "I've never seen anything like that before!"

"It's really cool," said Matthew. "Wait until you try it!"

Connor laughed. "I think I'll let someone else go first," he said.

It wasn't long before many children lined up to try out the Orbotron. One by one, they were strapped into the device. Then they laughed and screamed as they spun around in the sphere. Many of them got in line again for the second and third time.

Connor was having fun watching everyone. But his mood changed when he noticed the three boys at the next booth.

"Oh no!" said Connor, whispering to his friends,
"Trevor, Ronnie, and Zach are right next to us!"
"Just ignore them," said Lauren. Then she left
with Ryan and Stephanie to buy balloon animals.

Connor tried not to look at the three boys,
but he couldn't help himself. He noticed Trevor
and Zach were setting up soda pop bottles.
Ronnie was on a ladder painting a big, red sign.
It was going to read, "Bottle Ring Toss."

"Hey!" said Connor, nudging Matthew, "Look over there! They have a game—want to try it?"

"No way!" said Matthew. "I'm not going over there."

"Come on," said Connor. "Let's be nice to them. If it doesn't work, at least we tried."

Matthew sighed.

"Well, all right," he said, "I'll ask my Uncle Mike to be in charge while we're gone."

The two boys walked over to the next booth.

Zach saw them coming. "What do you guys want?" he asked.

"Well," said Connor, taking a dollar out of his pocket, "we'd like to play your game."

"The Bottle Ring Toss isn't for sissies," said Ronnie. "Get lost!"

"Yeah," added Trevor. "Beat it!" He took a step forward to shove Connor.

Just then, Trevor accidentally bumped the ladder that held the can of paint.

"Look out!" shouted Connor, pulling Trevor away
from the falling bucket.

The can hit the ground and splattered paint
everywhere! "Whoa!" said Trevor. "That was a close call!"

"It sure was!" said Matthew. "Connor saved you
from getting a big bump on your head. The paint can
would have hit you!"

"Trevor, I'm glad you're okay," Connor said.

He turned to Matthew. "Come on, let's go," he said.

Soon, Lauren and the others returned with some bad news.

"They just announced the winner for the best booth," she said.

"We didn't win the prize. They gave it to the girl who brought the jungle jump."

"Oh no!" said Connor. "Well, at least we made thirty-seven dollars today."

All of a sudden, someone tapped him on the shoulder. Connor turned to see Trevor standing behind him.

"I guess I should thank you for helping me today," said Trevor.

"It's okay," said Connor.

"I have a question for you," said Trevor. "Why would you want to help *me*? I've never done anything nice to you. Why didn't you just let the paint can fall on top of me?"

"Trevor, I don't hate you," said Connor. "I really
wish we could get along."

Trevor smiled. "Do you think you'd ever want to
be my friend?" he asked.

"Sure," said Connor. "I'll start by giving you and the guys a free ride on the Orbotron!"

"Thanks," said Trevor. "And your friends can try the Bottle Ring Toss!"

Later, Connor went with his friends to a table near the food stands.

"Well," he said, "we didn't win the prize, but some good things happened anyway. We made some money, but more importantly, we turned an enemy into a friend."

"It's been a fun day," said Ryan. "Hey! Let's go get a hot dog!"

"Good idea!" said Connor.